ROWAN AVA SKYE

The Axolotl's Saint Patrick's Day Parade

Copyright © 2025 by Rowan Ava Skye

All rights reserved. No part of this publication may be reproduced, stored or transmitted in any form or by any means, electronic, mechanical, photocopying, recording, scanning, or otherwise without written permission from the publisher. It is illegal to copy this book, post it to a website, or distribute it by any other means without permission.

This novel is entirely a work of fiction. The names, characters and incidents portrayed in it are the work of the author's imagination. Any resemblance to actual persons, living or dead, events or localities is entirely coincidental.

First edition

ISBN: 9798305790146

This book was professionally typeset on Reedsy.
Find out more at reedsy.com

Contents

Introduction	1
Chapter 1: Axel's Lucky Surprise	3
Chapter 2: The Rainbow That Vanished	6
Chapter 3: The Parade That Never Was	10
Chapter 4: The Leprechaun's Puzzle	15
Chapter 5: The Emerald Gatekeeper	19
Chapter 6: The Parade's Magical Secret	23
Afterword	27

Introduction

Axel the axolotl had never been one to chase after ordinary adventures. He didn't mind getting his little pink paws wet, exploring the deep corners of the stream or racing the wind on a crisp, sunny morning. But today—today was different. Today was Saint Patrick's Day, and Axel was determined to experience something truly magical.

In the heart of the emerald meadow where Axel lived, the air always seemed to sparkle a little brighter on Saint Patrick's Day. The leaves shimmered in a thousand shades of green, the earth hummed with life, and the distant hills seemed to glow with the promise of something wonderful. Axel had heard whispers of the great Saint Patrick's Day Parade, a celebration unlike any other, where the rainbow was said to lead to treasures beyond imagination.

But this year—this year, something felt off. As Axel swam through the cool stream, his pink-red gills fluttering with excitement, he couldn't shake the feeling that the parade wasn't going to be as it seemed.

It started when Axel noticed the first sign: a mysterious shamrock, unlike any he had ever seen before, floating in the water. It wasn't just any shamrock—it gleamed with a golden glow, as if it were calling to him, whispering a secret only he could hear. As Axel reached out to touch it, the ground beneath him trembled slightly, and a strange, tingling feeling ran through his body.

"Could this be the beginning of my adventure?" Axel wondered aloud, his eyes wide with curiosity.

What he didn't know, though, was that this shamrock was just the beginning of something far more extraordinary—something that would change his understanding of Saint Patrick's Day, magic, and friendship forever.

Axel wasn't sure what lay ahead. Was the shamrock merely a sign? Or did it hold a power greater than anything he could have imagined? There were whispers of rainbows that disappeared, of parades that never quite arrived, and of a grand treasure hidden somewhere in the midst of it all. But what kind of treasure? Gold? Fame? Or something more?

With the shamrock in his tiny hands, Axel set out on an unexpected journey. His heart beat faster with every step, and a thousand questions swirled in his mind. Where was the parade? What secrets did it hide? And why, despite all the magic surrounding Saint Patrick's Day, did Axel feel like he was about to stumble upon something even more mysterious than a pot of gold?

The real question was: Would Axel and his friends—Benny the bear, Tina the turtle, and Shelly the snail—be ready for the answers they were about to uncover?

But one thing was for certain: This wasn't going to be your typical parade. It was a parade full of surprises, twists, and the kind of magic that could make even the most ordinary day feel extraordinary.

So, if you're ready for the adventure of a lifetime, hold on tight, and join Axel and his friends. The Saint Patrick's Day Parade is about to begin—though no one knows where it might lead.

Chapter 1: Axel's Lucky Surprise

In the peaceful depths of the shimmering Emerald Stream, Axel the axolotl swam happily. His soft, pink skin glowed gently against the water, and his golden gills fluttered like delicate ribbons as he explored his favorite underwater world. Axel was always cheerful, and he loved discovering new, beautiful things hidden beneath the surface. But today, something was different. Today, something extraordinary was waiting for him.

It all started when Axel noticed a strange glimmer in the water, just past the sparkling river rocks he knew so well. It wasn't like the sunlight dancing on the water's surface—it was something brighter, something mysterious. Axel's curiosity took over. He swam toward the glow, his tiny tail flicking excitedly behind him.

As Axel drew closer, his eyes widened in wonder. There, nestled between a cluster of river stones, was an ancient-looking shamrock. Its leaves shimmered with an ethereal glow, a mix of emerald green and gold that seemed to pulse with magic. Axel blinked twice, unsure of what he was seeing. This wasn't like any shamrock he had ever seen. It wasn't just any lucky charm—it was *alive*.

"Wow..." Axel whispered to himself, reaching out one webbed paw to touch it. The moment his fingers brushed against the leaves, a warm, tingling sensation spread up his arm and through his entire body. The magic was real, and it was *powerful*.

Suddenly, the shamrock shifted in the water, its leaves spinning around in a circle. Axel gasped as the world around him seemed to warp and change.

Colors swirled in a whirlpool of greens, golds, and blues. A soft voice echoed in his ears, though no one was around.

"Axel... You have found the heart of the Saint Patrick's Day Parade."

Axel blinked in confusion. "The heart of the parade? What does that mean?" he asked aloud, his voice echoing softly in the stream.

The shamrock seemed to shimmer even brighter in response. A wave of magic spread out from it, creating a glowing path that twisted upward toward the surface of the water. Axel was mesmerized. Something told him that this shamrock wasn't just a lucky plant. It was a key—an invitation to something much bigger than he could imagine.

Without thinking, Axel followed the glowing path, swimming upwards toward the surface. As he breached the water, he found himself in a familiar meadow, but it looked different—magical, almost alive. The grass was greener than he had ever seen, and the air smelled fresh with the scent of wildflowers. It was as if the entire world around him was waiting for something wonderful to happen.

Then, Axel saw it—a large, golden sign that read: "Saint Patrick's Day Parade: The Grand Beginning."

"Wait a second..." Axel muttered. "It's *today*? I thought the parade wasn't for another week!"

But the sign glowed brightly, and Axel felt the magic in the air. Everything around him seemed to hum with excitement. As he looked closer, he noticed something strange. There was no parade. No floats, no banners, no people. The meadow was still and quiet.

"Where is everyone?" Axel wondered aloud.

The shamrock in his paw fluttered again, and a new voice—this time clearer—whispered:

"The parade has disappeared. Only you can bring it back, Axel. Your luck has led you here, but now, you must choose."

Axel's heart raced. What did that mean? How could he bring the parade back? He had always heard that Saint Patrick's Day was a celebration of joy, luck, and unity, but now the magical parade seemed lost, just like the shamrock that had brought him here.

CHAPTER 1: AXEL'S LUCKY SURPRISE

Before Axel could ask any more questions, the shamrock's golden glow faded, leaving behind a single clue—a tiny golden coin, glinting in the grass. Axel bent down and picked it up, marveling at its warmth and weight. As he did, a new wave of magic washed over him.

The voice returned, a little softer this time. "Follow the coins. They will lead you to where the parade's magic still lies, hidden in plain sight."

Axel looked at the golden coin in his paw, then up at the meadow ahead. Golden coins were scattered throughout the field, like breadcrumbs leading to a grand mystery. Axel smiled, his heart racing with excitement. This wasn't just about luck—it was about adventure.

With a deep breath, Axel took the first step onto the glowing path of golden coins, ready to solve the mystery and bring the Saint Patrick's Day Parade back to life.

But what Axel didn't know was that the parade he was about to uncover wasn't going to be anything like he expected. The magic behind it was far greater—and far more unpredictable—than anything he could imagine.

As Axel moved forward, the golden coins shimmered brighter, and the world around him seemed to come alive, whispering of secrets and surprises yet to come.

Would Axel be able to restore the parade? Or would the magic slip away forever? Only time would tell—but one thing was certain: his adventure had only just begun.

This chapter introduces the magical shamrock, setting the stage for Axel's unexpected adventure and a mystery that will unfold in the coming chapters. It leaves readers eager to know what will happen next while hinting at deeper magic and twists ahead.

Chapter 2: The Rainbow That Vanished

Axel and his friends were out on a bright, crisp morning in the meadow, the air filled with the promise of adventure. The golden glow of sunlight danced through the grass, and the sky was a flawless shade of blue—perfect for a stroll. Axel, the cheerful axolotl, bounced with excitement, his golden gills shimmering in the soft breeze. Beside him walked Benny the bear, whose big paws made deep impressions in the earth with each step, Tina the turtle, who moved slowly but always had the sharpest eye for detail, and Shelly the snail, who was always quiet but had a curious spark in her eyes.

The group was chatting merrily, sharing stories of the treasures they hoped to find when Axel suddenly stopped in his tracks, his eyes widening in awe.

"Look!" Axel shouted, pointing to the sky.

Everyone followed his gaze and gasped. A brilliant rainbow arced across the sky, stretching from one side of the meadow to the other. The colors were so vivid—reds, oranges, yellows, greens, blues, indigos, and violets—that it looked as if the rainbow had been painted with magic itself. The shimmering spectrum lit up the entire meadow in a dazzling array of colors.

"It's beautiful!" Tina exclaimed.

"Magical!" Benny added, his large eyes wide with wonder.

"It's like a bridge to another world," Shelly murmured, her eyes glinting.

But just as quickly as it had appeared, something strange happened. The rainbow started to flicker.

The colors began to blur, and then—*poof*—it vanished completely, leaving nothing but an empty sky.

CHAPTER 2: THE RAINBOW THAT VANISHED

"Where did it go?" Benny asked, his deep voice filled with confusion.

Axel's heart raced. "It disappeared... but how?" he said, looking around, hoping the rainbow would reappear. It didn't. There was no sign of it, not even a glimmer.

Tina squinted into the distance. "That's strange. I've never seen a rainbow vanish like that before. It was as if it was... sucked up by the sky."

"I've got a feeling this isn't just any ordinary rainbow," Axel said, his gills fluttering nervously. "It *had* to be magical."

The friends stood in silence for a moment, the quiet of the meadow suddenly feeling unsettling. Axel couldn't shake the feeling that the rainbow's disappearance was the start of something bigger. Something important.

Suddenly, Axel's paw brushed against something cold in the grass. He bent down to investigate and gasped. There, lying hidden beneath a patch of wildflowers, was a glowing, golden coin.

"Another one!" Shelly said. "Like the ones we saw earlier in the meadow."

Axel took the coin in his paw. The golden shimmer was unmistakable. It glowed with the same magical aura as the shamrock. This couldn't just be a coincidence. He held it up, and his friends crowded around.

"Where do you think this came from?" Benny asked.

Axel turned the coin over in his paw, inspecting it carefully. On the other side of the coin, there was a tiny engraving: a rainbow, half-faded, with the words, *Follow the colors. Find the truth.*

"Follow the colors? What does that mean?" Tina asked, scratching her head.

"I think we have to follow the rainbow—wherever it went," Axel said, his voice filled with determination.

The group of friends exchanged glances, and then, without another word, they set off together, following the faint shimmer of golden coins scattered across the meadow.

The search for the rainbow led the group into a thick forest, the trees towering above them like ancient guardians. The sunlight was dimmer now, and the air grew cool and heavy. It felt like the world had changed. The colors of the forest were more muted, as if the rainbow had taken all its brightness with it. Axel's heart pounded as he led the way, Benny, Tina, and Shelly close behind.

As they ventured deeper into the forest, the golden coins grew more frequent, but they also seemed to lead them in a winding path, one that grew more twisted and puzzling with each step. Axel's excitement turned to uncertainty. Why were the coins scattered in this strange pattern? Why did the rainbow disappear so mysteriously?

Suddenly, Axel stopped in his tracks. He had reached the edge of a clearing, and in the center, there stood a stone archway—old, worn, and covered in vines. But what caught Axel's attention was the faint shimmer of color rising from the arch.

The colors weren't quite a rainbow, but they were there—subtle shades of red, yellow, and blue. Axel could feel the magic in the air. This wasn't just an ordinary archway. It was the key to unlocking the mystery of the rainbow's disappearance.

Axel took a deep breath. "I think the rainbow's magic led us here."

He stepped forward, the others following closely behind. As soon as Axel crossed the threshold of the archway, a burst of colors exploded around him. A dazzling whirl of light and color enveloped the group. Axel could barely keep his eyes open, but he felt the magic flowing through him, and everything around him seemed to shift.

Then, with a sudden jolt, the light stopped. The clearing they had entered was gone. Instead, they were standing at the top of a great hill, overlooking a vast, sparkling landscape. In the distance, Axel could see a massive pot of gold sitting atop a small hill, gleaming brightly under the sun. But there was something unusual about this place—it was *different* from any world Axel had ever known. The sky was a deep violet, the grass a shade of silver, and strange glowing flowers bloomed in the air.

"This place... it's like another world," Shelly whispered.

"I think the rainbow didn't just disappear," Axel said, his voice full of awe. "It *led* us here. We were supposed to find this place."

Before anyone could say anything else, a soft voice echoed from the air.

"Welcome, travelers," the voice said. "You have found the hidden realm of the Rainbow's Secret. But only those pure of heart can uncover its truth. Are

CHAPTER 2: THE RAINBOW THAT VANISHED

you ready to continue?"

Axel's heart raced. He had no idea what was waiting for them in this mysterious land, but he knew one thing: their adventure was only just beginning. The rainbow had vanished, but its secrets were just beginning to unfold.

This chapter builds mystery and excitement while hinting at a greater magical journey ahead. It uses a sudden twist—leading the characters into an unfamiliar realm—to keep the readers intrigued and eager for the next step in Axel's adventure.

Chapter 3: The Parade That Never Was

The excitement had been building for days. Axel couldn't remember a time when he'd looked forward to something as much as he did the Saint Patrick's Day Parade. All of the animals in the meadow were buzzing with excitement. Axel had carefully prepared his festive green top hat, decorated with tiny golden clovers, and was practically bouncing with energy. His friends, Benny, Tina, and Shelly, had all joined in the preparations. Everyone was eager to celebrate the magical day of Saint Patrick.

The meadow had been transformed. Colorful banners fluttered in the breeze, and tables were loaded with delicious foods—green pies, clover-shaped cookies, and sparkling emerald drinks. The air smelled of sweet baked goods, and music echoed from every corner. Axel could hardly wait. The parade was the highlight of the day, a grand procession of floats, dancers, and performers that wound through the town and into the meadow. The floats were always decked out in gold, clovers, and rainbows.

"Are you ready, Axel?" Benny asked, his large paws gently tapping the ground. "The parade's about to start!"

Axel's gills fluttered in excitement. "I've been ready all week! Let's go!" He grabbed his hat and hurried toward the heart of the meadow where everyone gathered for the big event.

But when Axel arrived at the starting point of the parade, something was wrong.

There were no floats.

No streamers or decorated wagons.

No marching bands or dancers.

CHAPTER 3: THE PARADE THAT NEVER WAS

Just a handful of confused animals wandering around, looking just as puzzled as Axel felt.

"What's going on?" Axel murmured. He looked around at the empty meadow. The place where the parade was supposed to begin looked desolate. It wasn't like anything he'd seen before. There were no signs of preparations, no excited chatter, nothing.

Benny lumbered over, scratching his head. "Where's the parade? This is the first year it's not showing up on time."

Tina looked around nervously. "I've been looking forward to this all month. What's happening? Where did the parade go?"

Shelly, always the quiet observer, had been scanning the horizon. She slowly turned to Axel and whispered, "I think something's... wrong."

Axel's heart sank. He couldn't believe it. Saint Patrick's Day was always so full of life and fun, but now it seemed like the entire celebration had vanished. There was no sign of the grand parade, and the air, which was supposed to be filled with the sound of music and laughter, was unnervingly quiet.

"We need to figure out what happened," Axel said, determination building in his chest. "I won't let Saint Patrick's Day just disappear! Let's find out where the parade went."

The friends immediately set off in search of answers. They ventured through the meadow, past the empty tables and tents. They crossed the bridge that led into the nearby woods, hoping that they might find a clue. The more they searched, though, the more perplexed they became. The whole place felt wrong.

"This doesn't make any sense," Benny said, his deep voice tinged with frustration. "There's no trace of the floats. No parade route. Nothing!"

Axel stopped in his tracks. "Wait... I just thought of something. Remember that strange rainbow we saw earlier? Could it be connected to this?"

Tina blinked in confusion. "You think the rainbow and the parade are linked?"

"Maybe," Axel said. "The rainbow disappeared, but it might've taken something else with it—like the parade itself. Perhaps the magic of Saint Patrick's Day is tied to the rainbow. If the rainbow disappeared, maybe the parade did too!"

"Okay, so we're searching for a missing parade and a disappearing rainbow..." Shelly said slowly, "and we have no idea where they are."

Axel gave a small nod. "It's a bit of a mystery, but I'm sure we can solve it. We need to find the rainbow first, and the parade should follow. Let's keep going."

The friends trudged on, hoping to find some sign of the magical rainbow that had been so elusive before. They crossed meadows, climbed hills, and wandered deep into the forest, following the faint glimmers of gold coins scattered on the ground like breadcrumbs. But still, there was no sign of the rainbow.

Just when Axel was beginning to feel hopeless, Tina's voice rang out from up ahead.

"Look! I found something!"

Axel hurried over, his heart racing. Tina was standing in front of a thick patch of tall, swaying grass. She was holding something in her paw—a small golden key.

"This was hidden in the grass," Tina said, her eyes wide. "Do you think it's a clue?"

Axel took the key in his hand, turning it over and inspecting it closely. The surface gleamed in the sunlight, and something about it seemed to hum with magic. There was an engraving on the side—a symbol of a pot of gold surrounded by four-leaf clovers.

"This must be it!" Axel exclaimed. "This is the key we've been searching for. Let's see where it leads."

Without hesitation, the group followed the trail, the key feeling like it was guiding them, almost as if it had a mind of its own. They came to the base of an enormous tree, its trunk thick with age and its branches stretching far above. In front of the tree was a small wooden door, hidden amongst the roots. It was so well camouflaged by vines and flowers that Axel almost missed it.

"This is it! The door we need to open!" Axel said, his voice full of hope.

Benny reached down with his large paw and carefully inserted the key into the lock. With a loud click, the door swung open, revealing a tunnel

CHAPTER 3: THE PARADE THAT NEVER WAS

of shimmering light.

The tunnel seemed to stretch on forever, glowing with the same magical energy as the rainbow. Axel and his friends stepped inside, and the door shut behind them with a soft thud.

The further they walked, the more they felt like they were descending into a hidden world. The walls were adorned with glowing shamrocks and twinkling lights, and the air smelled sweet with the scent of clover. The path before them seemed to grow brighter with each step, leading them toward the heart of the hidden world.

At the end of the tunnel, Axel saw something that made his heart skip a beat: a massive, golden parade float, gleaming under the light. It was beautifully decorated with sparkling clovers and shamrocks, and atop it stood a grand figure holding a staff of gold—a leprechaun, grinning from ear to ear.

"Welcome, Axel," the leprechaun said, his voice warm and friendly. "You've found the parade, but it's been hidden away to protect the magic of Saint Patrick's Day."

Axel's eyes widened. "So the parade was hidden all along?"

The leprechaun nodded. "Aye. When the rainbow vanished, it caused a disturbance in the magic that makes Saint Patrick's Day so special. But thanks to your determination and cleverness, the parade can now return. You've saved the celebration, and the magic will live on!"

With a wave of the leprechaun's staff, the float came to life. It began to float out of the hidden chamber, rising through the tunnel and back into the meadow. Axel and his friends followed eagerly, watching in awe as the parade began to form around them. The music played again, the banners fluttered, and the float joined the others, parading through the meadow with joy.

And so, the Saint Patrick's Day Parade was back, brighter and more magical than ever before, thanks to Axel and his friends. The celebration continued with laughter and cheer, and Axel knew that this adventure would go down in the books as one of the most unforgettable Saint Patrick's Days ever.

In this chapter, Axel and his friends face an unexpected problem: the missing parade. As they work together to track it down, they uncover secrets about the magic of Saint Patrick's Day and the hidden world that protects it. The twist comes when they discover the parade had been hidden to preserve its magic, and they play a crucial role in bringing it back.

Chapter 4: The Leprechaun's Puzzle

Axel and his friends had barely caught their breath from the whirlwind of the missing parade when they noticed something unusual. As the grand Saint Patrick's Day Parade floated through the meadow, the air suddenly grew still. The laughter and music faded, and the vibrant colors of the parade began to lose their luster. The pot of gold at the head of the parade dimmed, and the four-leaf clovers scattered on the ground turned dull.

"What's happening?" Axel asked, a knot of worry forming in his stomach.

Benny, his large bear-like ears twitching, looked around. "This doesn't feel right. The parade's losing its magic."

Before anyone could speak, a soft chuckle echoed through the air, like a trickle of wind through the trees. Then, from the edge of the meadow, a figure appeared. Standing tall and proud in the midst of the fading parade was a small, mischievous leprechaun. His long green coat shimmered in the fading sunlight, and his eyes gleamed with a playful glint. A golden buckle gleamed on his hat, and his boots clicked as he made his way toward Axel and his friends.

"Hello, young adventurers," the leprechaun said, his voice rich with mischief. "I see you've found the parade—but there's one more challenge before you can continue your journey."

Axel stepped forward, a mix of excitement and suspicion in his heart. "A challenge? What do we need to do?"

The leprechaun's eyes twinkled. "Ah, that's the spirit! You see, this parade isn't just for fun. It holds the magic that keeps Saint Patrick's Day alive, and I'm afraid... the magic is slipping away."

Tina the turtle blinked, looking worried. "What do we have to do?"

"Simple," the leprechaun replied, his voice growing more serious. "To continue the parade, you must solve my riddle. But be warned—time is not on your side. You must crack the code before the sun sets, or the magic will fade forever."

Shelly, the wise snail, frowned. "A riddle? That's all?"

"Oh, it's not just any riddle," the leprechaun said with a wink. "It's a puzzle of magic, and only those with true courage and clever minds will solve it. Are you ready?"

Axel and his friends exchanged uncertain glances but nodded in unison. They'd come this far—they couldn't back down now.

"Very well," the leprechaun said, grinning as he raised a hand and a golden scroll appeared from thin air. The scroll unfurled itself, revealing the riddle written in elegant script. The leprechaun cleared his throat dramatically.

"Here's the riddle, my clever friends:"

"I am never seen but always there,
I have no voice, but I'm everywhere.
I can be felt when you're in need,
But when you chase me, I'll always recede.
What am I?"

Axel stared at the riddle, his brain working overtime to decipher its meaning. He could feel the weight of the moment—the sun was already lower in the sky, casting long shadows over the meadow. He had to solve this riddle before time ran out.

"Let's think this through," Axel said, tapping his chin with his paw. "It says, 'I am never seen but always there.' That sounds like something invisible..."

Tina the turtle squinted. "Could it be the wind? The wind is always around us, but we can't see it."

"Right!" Axel exclaimed. "The wind is everywhere, but it has no form, no voice—it's always there but never seen."

Benny scratched his head. "But when you chase the wind, it just blows away, so that fits the part about it always receding. It has to be the wind!"

Axel turned back to the leprechaun. "It's the wind! The answer's the wind!"

The leprechaun smiled, his eyes glinting with approval. "Well done, young adventurers! You've solved the riddle."

But just as Axel and his friends let out a collective sigh of relief, something unexpected happened.

The meadow seemed to shift beneath their feet. The ground trembled slightly, and a low hum filled the air. A swirl of green mist appeared in front of them, and with a sudden whoosh, the riddle was absorbed into the mist, vanishing completely. The leprechaun's grin faded, and his eyes narrowed with a hint of mischief.

"Not so fast, my friends," he said, his voice now full of teasing challenge. "I gave you the answer, but there's one more twist."

"What do you mean?" Axel asked, his heart racing as he looked around in confusion.

The leprechaun chuckled. "Ah, you solved my riddle, but now you'll need to pass one more test. You see, the wind isn't just a riddle—it's a guardian of the magic that holds the parade together. Only by truly understanding the wind can you restore its magic."

"What does that mean?" Shelly the snail asked, her small body trembling in confusion.

The leprechaun's eyes gleamed with amusement. "You've answered the riddle, but now you must prove your understanding of the wind. Listen closely."

Without warning, the leprechaun began to sing, his voice rising and falling in a strange, melodic tune. The air around them seemed to ripple, and Axel felt a strange sensation wash over him. The meadow around them seemed to come alive with the sounds of the wind, rustling the trees, whispering through the leaves. The air felt thick with magic.

"You must listen carefully to the wind," the leprechaun explained. "It holds the key to your next challenge. Follow its whispers, and you'll find what's been hidden."

Axel furrowed his brow. What was the leprechaun trying to tell them? How could they "listen" to the wind?

The wind swirled around them, carrying faint voices that Axel couldn't quite understand. He focused harder, closing his eyes and listening with all his might. There—beneath the rustling leaves—he heard it: a soft, distant voice calling out, faint and clear.

"Find the four-leaf clover," the voice whispered. "It's the key to restoring the magic."

Axel's eyes flew open. "The four-leaf clover! That's what the wind's saying! It's the key!"

The leprechaun smiled, his eyes twinkling. "You've figured it out, young adventurer. The four-leaf clover holds the last piece of Saint Patrick's Day magic. Find it, and you'll restore the magic to the parade."

Axel's heart raced as the wind began to swirl faster, lifting the leaves off the ground and guiding him toward a small patch of grass at the edge of the meadow. There, hidden among the clovers, was a single, perfect four-leaf clover, glowing faintly with a golden light.

Axel knelt down, his heart racing with excitement. He carefully plucked the clover from the ground, feeling the magic surge through him. The moment his fingers touched the clover, the meadow came alive with color and sound. The parade floats shone brighter, the music began to play, and the animals cheered as the magic of Saint Patrick's Day was fully restored.

"Congratulations," the leprechaun said, his voice full of pride. "You've completed the puzzle and proven your worth. The parade is back, and the magic lives on."

With that, the leprechaun disappeared into the breeze, leaving Axel and his friends to bask in the glow of their success. The parade continued, brighter and more magical than ever, and Axel knew that they had truly earned their place in the celebration.

In this chapter, Axel and his friends solve a tricky riddle from a mischievous leprechaun, only to discover that they must listen to the wind and follow its whispers to restore the magic. The twist comes when they realize that the true key to the parade's magic is a single, glowing four-leaf clover, and they must work together to find it before time runs out. Through cleverness, teamwork, and listening to the world around them, they succeed in bringing the magic back to life.

Chapter 5: The Emerald Gatekeeper

The sun hung low in the sky as Axel and his friends trudged through the meadow, their excitement building with each step. The parade was moving forward, but they knew that something even greater awaited them. After the riddle of the leprechaun and the discovery of the four-leaf clover, Axel felt that they were getting closer to the heart of Saint Patrick's Day magic. But little did they know, their journey was far from over.

As they approached the edge of the meadow, the air grew cooler, and a soft mist began to swirl around their feet. The trees ahead seemed to grow taller and more ancient, their trunks thick and gnarled, their leaves shimmering in various shades of emerald green. Axel squinted into the fog, feeling the hairs on his back stand up. There was something strange about this forest—it wasn't just any ordinary woodland. This was a place where magic breathed through the leaves and hummed in the air.

"Is this... the enchanted forest?" Tina the turtle asked, her voice filled with awe.

"It must be," Shelly the snail replied, her eyes scanning the surroundings. "I've read about it in stories—the one that leads to the final destination of the Saint Patrick's Day Parade. But there's something strange about it. It feels like we're being watched."

Axel nodded, his heart pounding. He could sense it too—a presence, unseen but undeniable, watching their every move. And before they could take another step, a low, deep voice echoed through the trees, sending a chill down their spines.

"Who dares to enter the Emerald Forest?"

Startled, the group looked around. At first, they saw nothing but the mist and the towering trees. But then, as if materializing out of thin air, a figure appeared. Tall and regal, cloaked in a flowing robe of glittering emerald, stood a creature that neither Axel nor his friends had ever seen before. The figure's face was hidden beneath a hood, but its eyes shone with a bright, piercing green, like two glowing orbs in the darkness. A staff made of twisted silver and emerald stone rested in the creature's hand, and a crown of leaves adorned its head.

"I am the Emerald Gatekeeper," the figure intoned, its voice echoing through the forest like the wind in the trees. "Only those worthy may pass into the magical land where the parade's final destination lies. But to do so, you must prove your worth."

Axel stepped forward, feeling both nervous and determined. "We want to continue the parade, to restore the magic of Saint Patrick's Day. Please, let us pass."

The Emerald Gatekeeper studied Axel and his friends for a long moment before speaking again. "To pass, you must face a challenge. Each of you must choose a test that will prove your heart's true intention. If you succeed, the gates shall open. Fail, and you will be lost forever in this enchanted forest."

Shelly the snail's antennae twitched. "A test? What kind of test?"

"You will each face a trial based on your deepest fears or desires," the Gatekeeper explained. "Only those who can conquer their inner struggles will be worthy to pass."

The forest seemed to grow still at the mention of the trials, and the air seemed to thicken with magic. Axel's heart raced. What kind of tests would they face? Were they truly ready for this?

The Gatekeeper raised its staff, and a swirl of emerald light enveloped the group. "You will each step forward one at a time," it said. "Each trial will be unique. Choose wisely, for the forest will reflect your innermost self."

Axel took a deep breath and stepped forward, his mind spinning with uncertainty. The moment he moved, the mist around him parted, revealing a strange, winding path leading into a dense thicket. At the end of the path, Axel saw something that made his heart skip a beat: a tall, golden gate,

CHAPTER 5: THE EMERALD GATEKEEPER

its surface glimmering in the sunlight. But standing before the gate was a terrifying figure—an enormous shadowy creature, its eyes glowing red. It was a fearsome, dark version of Axel, towering and menacing, its fangs sharp and glistening.

"This is your fear, Axel," a voice whispered in the wind. "Face your own darkness, and prove you have the strength to move beyond it."

Axel froze. This dark version of himself—it was everything he feared. It represented his self-doubt, his insecurities. For years, Axel had wondered if he was truly worthy, if he could be the brave leader his friends saw him as. And now, here it was, in the form of the monster before him. The voice in his mind grew louder, telling him he couldn't do it, that he was too weak.

But then he remembered the journey he had already been through. The riddles, the puzzles, the magic. He had faced countless challenges and had never given up. This was no different. With newfound resolve, Axel lifted his chin and stepped forward, his voice steady as he spoke.

"You're not me. You're just my fear. And I can beat you."

The creature roared, its shadowy form lashing out toward Axel, but Axel stood firm, focusing on the light in his heart. He remembered the kindness, the strength, and the courage he'd shown on his adventure. The creature faltered, its form beginning to flicker and fade. Axel reached out his hand, touching the creature's chest, and in an instant, it dissolved into a puff of smoke. The golden gate shimmered brightly, and Axel could feel the magic of the forest responding to his victory.

"You've done it, Axel," the Gatekeeper's voice echoed. "You have faced your fear and overcome it."

Axel turned back to his friends, who were now ready to face their own trials. He nodded to them, his heart swelling with pride.

Next was Benny, who stepped forward with determination, but as soon as he walked into the mist, the air changed. The path twisted, and he found himself in a vast, dark forest, filled with thick shadows. The sounds of distant growls echoed around him, and Benny could feel his muscles tense. He was not afraid of the dark, but he was afraid of one thing: failure. The thought of not living up to the expectations of others, of letting down his friends, was what terrified him most.

"Benny, face your fear," the voice whispered. "Do you have the strength to overcome it?"

Benny stood tall, shaking his head. "I won't fail. Not today."

He marched through the forest, determined to find his way. His fear of failure haunted him, but his love for his friends—and the belief in himself—propelled him forward. He reached the end of the path and found the golden gate waiting for him. With a roar of victory, the shadows melted away, and the gate opened, allowing Benny to pass.

Next, Tina the turtle entered the mist, followed by Shelly the snail. Each of them faced their own fears and emerged victorious, proving that they were ready for whatever lay ahead. Finally, the group was united once more in front of the gate.

The Emerald Gatekeeper watched them with a mixture of admiration and approval. "You have proven your worth," the Gatekeeper said. "You are ready to enter the magical land where the parade's final destination lies."

With a flick of the Gatekeeper's staff, the gates swung open, revealing a path that led into a land beyond imagination—vibrant, magical, and full of wonder. Axel and his friends stepped forward, knowing that they had passed the test and were one step closer to their ultimate goal. The parade was waiting for them, and they were ready to face whatever came next.

In this chapter, Axel and his friends face the mysterious Emerald Gatekeeper, who challenges each of them to confront their deepest fears. Through determination, self-belief, and courage, they overcome their trials, proving their worth and earning the right to enter the final destination of the Saint Patrick's Day Parade. The twist comes when each of them has to face a version of their fears, leading to moments of personal growth and strength before they are allowed to continue their journey.

Chapter 6: The Parade's Magical Secret

After a long and eventful journey, Axel and his friends had finally arrived at the heart of the Saint Patrick's Day Parade. The air was filled with excitement as colorful floats and cheerful music echoed throughout the land. Axel's heart raced as he looked around, knowing that they were on the cusp of uncovering the final mystery—the grand finale of the parade. But there was something about this moment that made his excitement mix with an uneasy feeling. Something was… off.

The vibrant rainbow that had once disappeared now reappeared, stretching across the sky like a magical bridge leading to a distant land. The golden pot at the end of the rainbow glimmered brighter than ever before, as if it held the promise of a great treasure. Axel could feel the pull of it, drawing him closer, but there was also an inexplicable hesitation in his heart.

Axel, Benny the bear, Tina the turtle, and Shelly the snail walked toward the parade's grand finale, where all the magical festivities seemed to gather. Everywhere, there were leprechauns dancing, fairies flying, and lucky clovers shining like stars in the sky. The grand float, the centerpiece of the parade, stood towering before them. It was a magnificent, glimmering chariot made of emerald leaves, surrounded by sparkling four-leaf clovers. At the center of the float, a large golden cauldron bubbled with mysterious, shimmering liquid.

"This is it!" Axel said, his voice filled with awe. "The finale! We've made it!"

But as Axel looked closer, he noticed something strange. The parade seemed to have no end—no destination. The golden cauldron was glowing brighter, yet the closer they got, the more it seemed as though they were walking in circles. There were no people in sight—no other participants in the parade. No laughter or cheers. Only the soft bubbling of the cauldron.

"What's going on?" Tina asked, her voice trembling. "This isn't what we expected. There's no one here. Where did everyone go?"

Axel frowned. He had anticipated a grand celebration, a jubilant ending to their quest. But instead, the parade seemed stuck in time, repeating itself like a loop that went nowhere. The rainbow shimmered in the sky above them, but there was no end in sight.

Shelly the snail's antennae twitched nervously. "It feels like we've stepped into a different realm. Something isn't right."

Before Axel could respond, a sudden gust of wind blew through the clearing, and the golden cauldron began to tremble. The shimmering liquid inside it began to swirl, forming intricate patterns of light that danced around the group. Axel's heart raced as the liquid began to rise, forming into the shape of a glowing figure.

The figure hovered before them, its form made entirely of light, radiating warmth and power. It was neither a fairy nor a leprechaun. It had the graceful form of a spirit, with wings that shimmered like stardust. Its face was obscured by a veil of glowing mist, but its voice rang clear and full of wisdom.

"You have come far, little ones," the spirit spoke, its voice echoing like the wind through trees. "But the parade you seek... the celebration you yearn for... is not what you think it is."

Axel stepped forward, his heart pounding in his chest. "What do you mean? We've been on a journey to restore the magic of Saint Patrick's Day. The parade, the rainbow, the pot of gold—it's all been part of the adventure!"

The spirit nodded slowly. "Yes, you've seen the magic, and you've solved the riddles. But the true meaning of Saint Patrick's Day, the true magic, is not in the gold or the celebrations you've been chasing. The parade you sought... is not the one that leads to a treasure of riches. The treasure you seek is within you."

Benny the bear scratched his head, confused. "But... we've been following the rainbow, the float, the gold! Isn't that what Saint Patrick's Day is about?"

CHAPTER 6: THE PARADE'S MAGICAL SECRET

The spirit smiled softly, its wings fluttering. "Saint Patrick's Day is not just about riches or the festivities. It is about unity, kindness, and the spirit of giving. The magic you seek is not found in gold or leprechauns, but in the hearts of those who celebrate the day, in the joy of being together, and in the kindness you show to others."

Axel's mind was spinning. "So, what does this mean for us? We've come all this way... does that mean there's no pot of gold at the end of the rainbow?"

The spirit's eyes glowed brighter as it floated closer. "The pot of gold, the rainbow—it's a symbol. It's not about material wealth. It's about the bond you share with your friends, the love you have for one another. That is the true treasure. The parade you were chasing was only a reflection of your journey together, and the real magic was in the friendships you forged along the way."

A wave of realization washed over Axel. He looked around at Benny, Tina, and Shelly. They had been together through every trial, every puzzle, every moment of doubt. Their journey had not been about the destination—it had been about the growth they experienced as friends, as a team. The magic of Saint Patrick's Day was not something you could hold in your hands. It was something you carried in your heart.

"But why the cauldron? Why the parade?" Axel asked, still trying to make sense of everything.

The spirit answered gently, "The parade, the cauldron, and the rainbow—they are all symbols of the magic that lies within each person. The cauldron's glowing liquid is not gold, but the light of hope and love that shines within us. The rainbow is not a physical bridge, but a path that leads to understanding and joy. And the parade is not a procession of floats, but a celebration of the journey you've all taken together."

Axel's heart swelled with a mixture of emotions—relief, joy, and a sense of wonder. He looked at his friends, and they shared the same realization. They had been searching for something outside themselves, something tangible. But what they had truly been seeking was the bond they shared, the love that had guided them through every twist and turn.

"So... what happens now?" Shelly asked, her voice filled with awe.

The spirit smiled, and the golden cauldron's glow intensified, casting a warm light across the meadow. "Now, you return to the parade, not as seekers of gold, but as bearers of the true magic of Saint Patrick's Day. The parade's finale is not a destination—it is a reminder that the true treasure lies in the love and friendship you carry with you, and in the joy you spread to others."

The spirit slowly began to fade, its light dissipating like morning mist. The golden cauldron's glow softened, and the rainbow above began to shimmer gently, as though inviting the group to return.

Axel turned to his friends, his heart filled with gratitude. "We've got it. The parade is not about what we find at the end—it's about how we celebrate and share what we've learned with others."

The float before them glowed with new meaning, and the sounds of the parade began to return, the laughter, the music, and the celebration of friendship and love. Axel, Benny, Tina, and Shelly joined the parade once more, not seeking treasure, but sharing the true magic of the day with everyone they met.

As they marched through the meadow, the rainbow above them seemed to glow brighter, not with gold, but with the light of their newfound understanding. And in that moment, Axel knew that the Saint Patrick's Day Parade was more than just an event—it was a celebration of life, friendship, and the magic that bound them all together.

In this chapter, Axel and his friends uncover the true magic behind Saint Patrick's Day—the bonds of love and friendship, and the joy of celebrating together. The twist reveals that the treasure they sought was never gold, but the realization that the true meaning of the parade lies in the connections they share. The golden cauldron and rainbow become symbols of the light and magic that resides within each person, and the parade itself is a reflection of the love and kindness that makes the world magical.

Afterword

Thank you, dear reader, for joining Axel and his friends on this magical adventure! We hope you enjoyed every twist and turn of the journey, from the mysterious shamrock to the secrets of the Saint Patrick's Day Parade. It was a joy to have you alongside Axel as he uncovered the true meaning of friendship, magic, and celebration.

But don't worry, the adventure doesn't stop here! Be sure to check back soon for more stories, as we'll be bringing you even more enchanting tales in the coming days. There's a whole series of wonderful adventures just waiting for you, perfect for holidays, celebrations, and special moments with your loved ones. Whether it's a grand festive parade or the warmth of a holiday gathering, there's always a magical story to share!

We'd love for you to explore our other books in the series and enjoy more of the enchanting adventures that bring joy to readers of all ages. Axel and his friends will be back in new tales full of surprises and delightful moments—so stay tuned!

If you enjoyed this story, be sure to check out more heartwarming tales from Rowan Ava Skye. Perfect for gifts to family and friends, these stories will bring smiles, laughter, and the magic of the seasons to life, one page at a time.

Until next time, may your days be full of adventure and your heart full of joy.
With gratitude,
Rowan Ava Skye

Made in United States
North Haven, CT
18 January 2025